For Caz

First U.S. edition 1996

Library of Congress Cataloging-in-Publication Data

Vulliamy, Clara.
Ellen and Penguin and the new baby / Clara Vulliamy.—1st U.S. ed.
Summary: Ellen and her stuffed toy, Penguin, have difficulty
adjusting to a new baby brother.
ISBN 1-56402-697-3 (alk. paper)
[1. Brothers and sisters—Fiction.   2. Babies—Fiction.
3. Penguins—Fiction.]   I. Title
PZ7.V994En   1996
[E]—dc20   95-16164

2 4 6 8 10 9 7 5 3 1

Printed in Italy

This book was typeset in M Ehrhardt.
The pictures were done in watercolor.

Candlewick Press
2067 Massachusetts Avenue
Cambridge, Massachusetts 02140

ELLEN
AND
PENGUIN
AND THE NEW BABY

CLARA VULLIAMY

CANDLEWICK PRESS
CAMBRIDGE, MASSACHUSETTS

Ellen had a new baby brother.

Penguin wasn't sure if he liked
new baby brothers much.

Everywhere Ellen and Penguin went,

the baby came too.

When they wanted a quiet story,
the baby started crying.

And because Mom
was too busy to
help them,

a lot went
wrong.

The baby got Ellen's old mobile
with the woolly sheep hanging down.

"Penguin's mad," said Ellen.

"He really likes that mobile."

Ellen and Penguin got into the baby's
bassinet and pretended it was a little boat
taking them far out to sea.

"You'd better get out
or you'll break it," said Mom.

In the night,
Penguin
couldn't
sleep.

So Ellen had to bring him downstairs
and walk around and around with him,
patting his back.

The next morning, everyone was tired. Mom said, "What we need is a nice day out. Where should we go?" Ellen chose the park with the farm animals.

Ellen and Penguin were so
excited they ran all the
way down the path to
where the animals lived.

They saw some lambs and
a family of little startled chicks.

Penguin's favorites were the
snuffly piglets with curly tails.

Ellen liked the baby rabbits
snuggling together in the grass.

While Mom was unpacking the lunch,
the baby started crying again.
"Could you try and cheer him up?" said Mom.

Penguin wasn't sure what
to do, but Ellen said,
"Poor baby."

They tried a rattle
from his bag,

and a bear
and a book,
but he kept
on crying.

Then Penguin did a little dance.

The baby stopped crying and looked.

Ellen and Penguin danced
around and around and got
more and more dizzy.

They collapsed in a
heap, laughing.

And the baby joined in.

"Our baby loves us," said Ellen.

And they both agreed that new baby

brothers weren't so bad after all.